YO, HUNGRY WOLF!

DAVID VOZAR

YO, HUNGRY

ILLUSTRATED BY BETSY LEWIN

WOLF! A NURSERY RAP

A DOUBLEDAY BOOK FOR YOUNG READERS

A Doubleday Book for Young Readers
Published by
Delacorte Press
Bantam Doubleday Dell Publishing Group, Inc.
666 Fifth Avenue
New York, New York 10103
Doubleday and the portrayal of an anchor with a dolphin are trademarks of
Bantam Doubleday Dell Publishing Group, Inc.
Text copyright © 1993 by David Vozar
Illustrations copyright © 1993 by Betsy Lewin

Library of Congress Cataloging in Publication Data
Vozar, David.
Yo, hungry wolf! : a nursery rap / David Vozar ; illustrated by Betsy Lewin.
    p.   cm.
   "A Doubleday Book for Young Readers."
   Summary: A retelling in rap verse of "The Three Little Pigs," "Little Red
Riding Hood," and "The Boy Who Cried Wolf."
   ISBN 0-385-30452-8
   1. Fairy tales.   [1. Fairy tales.   2. Folklore.   3. Stories in rhyme.]
I. Lewin, Betsy, ill.   II. Title.
PZ8.3.V898Yo   1993
398.2 — dc20   [E]   91-46264   CIP   AC

The illustrations in this book were done in watercolors.
The text of this book is set in 16 point ITC Garamond Book Condensed.
Typography by Lynn Braswell.
Manufactured in the United States of America

April 1993

10 9 8 7 6 5 4 3 2 1

THIS BOOK IS DEDICATED WITH LOVE TO MY DAUGHTER, ARIANE.
—D.V.

YO, GUSTAVE DORÉ!
—B.L.

This here's the tale of a wolf that was hungry—
    had a swollen stomach all hollow and spongy.
Went to the barnyard lookin' for eats,
    and spied three pigs all juicy and sweet.
So he jumps the fence to grab and surprise 'em,
    but they see him and flee him with a speed that belies 'em.

Now, the wolf ain't fakin',
And his stomach is achin'.
He's got to have pigs
To slice into bacon.

He runs to a shack, pig hiding place of sticks.
　　He'll blow it down easy for his pork-chop fix.
He blows and he blows and the sticks, they cave in.
　　This pig is a goner and it's time to move in.
But before Wolfie grabs him, gets the pig in his jaw,
　　This one shoots past him to the house made of straw.

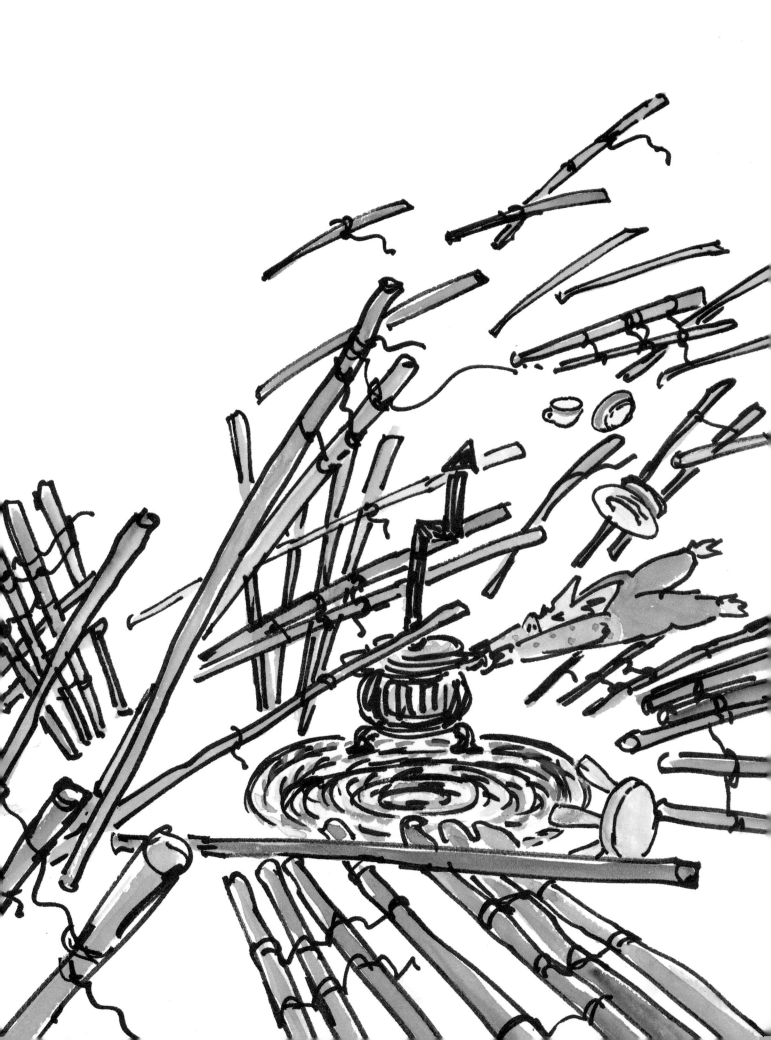

Two pigs are at bay
In the shack made of hay.
If the wolf blows it down,
It's barbecue day.

He goes to their house. Now he's really getting tired.
  But the thought "ham on rye" gets him reinspired.
He blows at his foes till his lungs feel all tattered.
  The pigs feel exposed 'cause their house has been scattered.
Wolfie chases his prey, soon dinner he'll be hoggin'.
  But he can't keep up with the pigs' jetlike joggin'.

Three pigs are hidin'.
Their time they are bidin'.
Safe in house made of brick
With aluminum sidin'.

Wolfie decides to give it one more chance.
   He sucks up air, almost bustin' his pants.
He lets out the air at the door with a roar,
   but the shack is intact as he slumps to the floor.
Wolfie's plumb tuckered out and the pigs dance about—
   'Cause they won't get roasted with apples in their snouts.

Pigs celebratin',
The wolf they're beratin'.
But he's got a plan
For house infiltratin'.

Paw over paw Wolfie climbs up the shack
　　To slide down the chimney in a sneak swine attack.
Halfway down clothes are soilin', and Wolfie's recoilin'.
　　In the fireplace below, the pigs' soup is boilin'.
He pops out the chimney, hits the ground with a *boink*.
　　The pigs shout, "Yahoo!" but it sounds more like *oink*.

So the pigs are the winners
And the wolf's feeling thinner.
So he'll check out Grandma's
To see what's for dinner.

LITTLE RED

Wolves everywhere, you know me,
The meanest wolf in history!
No one warned me when I saw this girl
Down the block all sweetness and curls.

I decided to pursue her, went right up to her.
Asked where she was going, my plan to subdue her.
Said she was going to Granny's with a basketful of goodies,
Had a long way to travel through pines, vines, and woodies.

Now, I hadn't eaten in many, many days.
I was walking around in a mean, hungry haze.
So I had to do something. I couldn't be lazy.
If I didn't eat soon, I knew I'd go crazy.

I got this idea and ran off quick.
Took my own little shortcut through leaves, grass, and stick.
I put feet to ground and then ground to feet—
When I finally got to Granny's, the girl I had beat.

Now, I know this seems like a happy wolf story,
But keep listening to me, 'cause it gets pretty gory.
I opened the door and saw Granny there—
Felt a bump on my head as I was hit with a chair.

I found out grannies can be mighty rough.
Though weak in physique they're really quite tough.
But I finally tired the old granny out
And locked her in the closet to muffle her shout.

I needed a disguise to change head to toes—
Now, I know this sounds silly, but I put on her clothes!
As I relaxed in her nightgown before beginning my chase,
I was feeling sort of pretty in the old lady's lace.

There was a knock on the door—it had to be the girl.
I leapt across the floor and into bed with a twirl.
Pulled the covers up fast, all the way to my eyes,
Feeling pretty silly in my granny disguise.

As the girl walked in she pulled off her hood.
Had a pang in my stomach, this would come to no good.
This was not *any* girl I had met in the wood—
I was trifling with Little Red Rappinghood.

She said, "Yo, wily wolf! I see through your disguise.
You're not my granny, I can tell by your eyes.
Your eyes are the size of those mean wolf guys
Who hide in beds, so don't tell me no lies."

I was taken aback by Little Red's attack.
It took several seconds before I could react.
I said, "I am your granny, but my eyes are swollen.
They were stung by a bee while I was out strollin'."

Red said, "No, you're not, you lie a lot.
Just look at the size of those ears you've got.
They're all hairy and scary and very, very long.
Don't say you're my granny, 'cause I'll tell you, you're wrong."

One more time I tried to ad lib.
I sat for a moment and thought up this fib —
"I am your granny, but the winds can be bold,
So I wear these earmuffs to keep out the cold."

"If you're my granny, then why the big nose?"
Little Red said, accusing as she sat on my toes.
"Don't tell me it's cold or you've been stung by a bee,
'Cause my granny's nose is the size of a flea."

I said, "I know it's big," as I faked a sob.
"I tried to improve it with a fancy nose job.
When they took off the bandage and I looked at my face,
I was sad and mad, how my nose was disgraced."

Red said, "The stories you tell are beyond belief.
I know you're a wolf, just look at your teeth —
They're long and sharp, not short and round,
And you look foolish and *ugly* in Granny's nightgown."

As a wolf I just couldn't take no more—
I leapt out of bed, and Red ran to the door.
I said, "Get out of here quick before my temper blows,
I may *not* be your granny, but I look *good* in her clothes."

Red ran away, and I thought that was that,
And went to the wardrobe to try on a hat.
Heard a horrible sound and turned around—
'Twas the sound of the door crashing down to the ground.

A woodsman came in—swung an ax at me—
There was no time for thinking, only to flee.
This guy was as big as a big ocean whale,
And he just kept on swinging, almost getting my tail.

I ran out the door, still in Granny's dress,
Everything seemed a blur in this time of distress.
Little Red was there to get the last word.
To me, at the time, it sounded absurd.

She said, "Wolfie, you'd better change your diet—
Eat anything else, steam it or fry it.
'Cause girls and grannies aren't meant to be eaten.
If you try it again, you'll just get a beatin.'"

So wolves everywhere, hear what I'm confessin',
Pay attention to me and learn your lesson.
Since meeting Little Red, I've been in a daze.
It took me a while, but I'm changing my ways.

Now when I walk down the street, I'm not booed.
I don't chase no one, 'cause I'm eatin' junk food.
No more little girls or grannies for me—
It's dunkin' cookies in coffee or donuts in tea!

THE BOY WHO CRIED WOLF

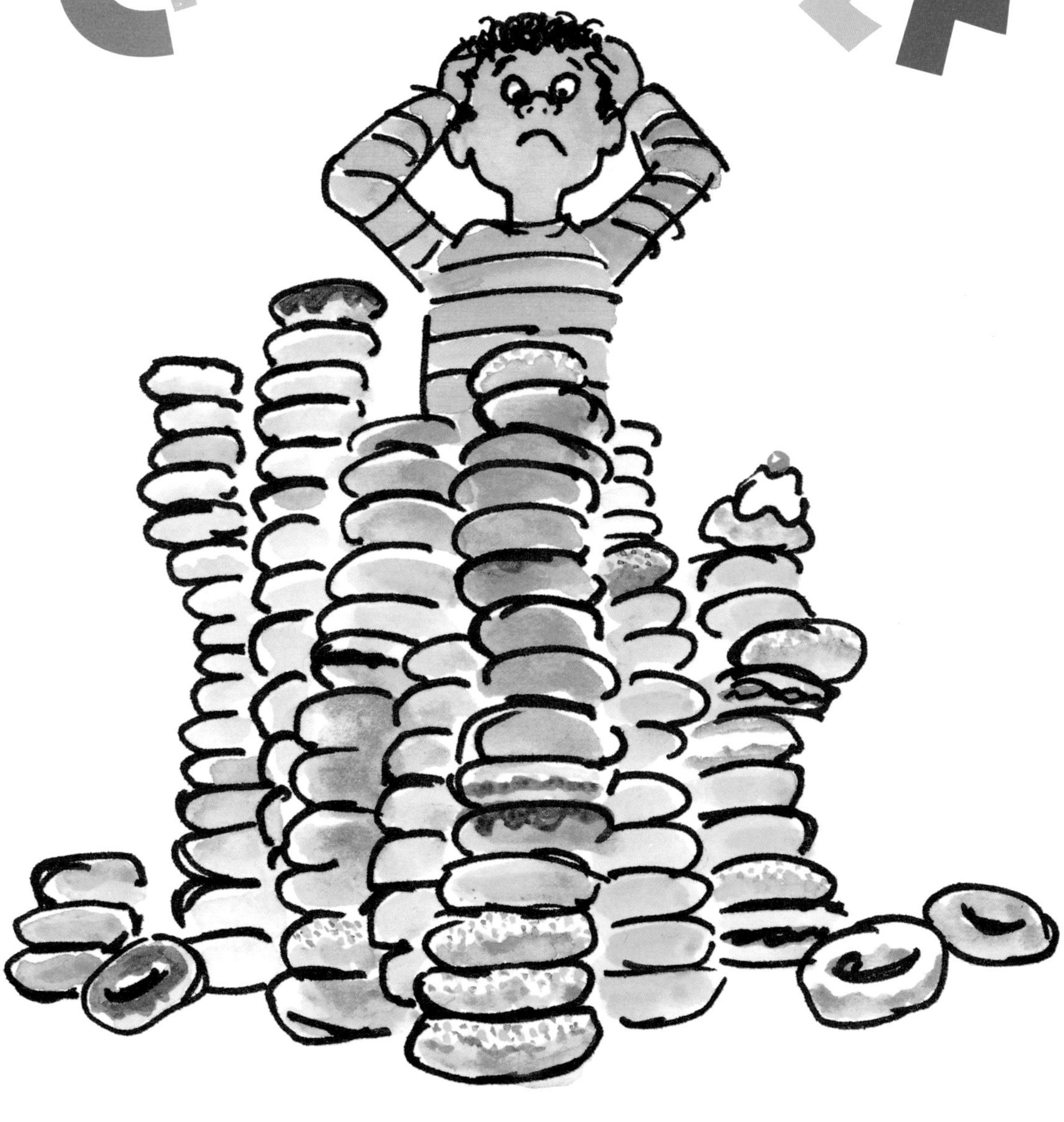

There's a shop down the street
Where a boy sells donuts, tart and sweet.
Coconut, vanilla, chocolate with cherries,
Plain with holes, filled up with berries.

Business has been slow at the shop—
The passersby, they just won't stop.
They whiz on by, off to work they go.
It's bringing the boy financial woe.

The boy sat and thought, he wondered about it.
Then he got an idea and decided to shout it.
In an effort to grab the smart donut buyer,
He opened the door and screamed out, "Fire!"

People came running into the store,
Off the sidewalk and through the door.
Everyone said, "Hey, where's the smoke?"
But the boy just laughed at his little joke.

He said, "Look, there are no flames,
This is just one of my little games
To get you here to buy my treats
Before you go back into the streets."

"There's no way now we'll buy your wares,"
The crowd said, giving him angry stares.
They were mad at the joke he'd played.
Everyone left, no one delayed.

They went away, wouldn't buy a thing—
Not a corn muffin, not a jelly ring.
The boy needed a way to bring them in again,
And he'd mark down the price—one free with ten.

He gave a thought, but the time was brief.
He ran to the door and he yelled, "Stop, thief!"
People came from every direction
To his shop of sweet confection.

They said, "Where is the one that did the stealin'?"
Then the boy blushed with an uneasy feelin'.
Said, "I was just kidding, I wasn't robbed,"
As he backed away from the angry mob.

The boy just shook, his face went pale.
Once again, he feared, there'd be no sale.
He stood alone there in his store
With donuts piled up, ceiling to floor.

"Pardon me for interrupting this rhyme,
But I've been off these pages, biding my time.
Throughout this book I've had barely a meal,
But this bakery story could be a good deal."

The wolf walked in and closed the door.
The boy was scared right to the core.
He said, "Stay away or I'll scream."
The wolf grabbed an éclair filled with cream.

He said, "Go ahead. Yell real, real loud.
Go ahead, cry out for a crowd.
Folks won't come—and your donuts I'll be takin'—
'Cause they won't believe you, they'll think you're fakin'."

Wolfie ate and ate, till he could eat no more
As the boy cried for help out the door.
When the wolf was done, nothing left to do,
He walked away, leaving the little boy blue.

Later on, the boy would tell what happened
When Wolfie ate his donuts, all the while rappin'.
He said, "I'm not lyin', I'm not deceivin'."
But the people just laughed, no one believed him.

And the wolf went home and got into bed
With visions of donuts still in his head.
Under his quilts, all warm and cozy,
He was filled with happiness—from head to toesies.

He thought of his day and the things that he did—
Of chasing pigs and Granny's bed where he hid.
Little Red, the axman, the boy now in sorrow—
He wondered how he'd get his three squares tomorrow.